I love you fluidly
like water
meets land.

I love you openly
like the sky.

I love you sociably like a seagull's cry.

I love you freshly
like salty spray.

I love you smoothly
like a ray.

I love you splashily like the spout of a whale.

I love you flexibly
like a seahorse's tail.

I love you joyfully
like a seal.

I love you electrically
like an eel.

I love you shiftingly
like a dune.

I love you subtly like the daytime moon.

I love you
protectively
like a tube of
sunscreen.

I love you airtightly
like a submarine.

I love you patiently
like a snail.

I love you brightly
like a pail.

I love you snappily like a crab's claws.

I love you widely like a shark's jaws.

I love you
energetically like a
crashing wave.

I love you
unchartedly like an
undersea cave.

I love you swimmingly
like a fish.

I love you unbreakably
like a picnic dish.

I love you brightly
like the sun.

I love you bouncily
like beach ball fun.

I love you geometrically
like a shell.

I love you
distinctly like that
low-tide smell.

I love you breezily
like a sailing boat.

I love you markedly
like a lobster float.

I love you pliably
like marram grass.

I love you
uncommonly like
blue sea glass.

I love you predictably like the tide.

I love you awesomely like a sweet, sweet ride.

I love you beachly, oceanly, shorely.